845275

LEWIS CARROLL

THROUGH THE LOOKING–GLASS

AND WHAT ALICE FOUND THERE

ABRIDGED & ILLUSTRATED BY
TONY ROSS

Atheneum · 1993 · New York

Maxwell Macmillan Canada
Toronto

Maxwell Macmillan International
New York   Oxford   Singapore   Sydney

Atheneum
Macmillan Publishing Company
866 Third Avenue
New York, NY 10022

Maxwell Macmillan Canada, Inc.
1200 Eglinton Avenue East
Suite 200
Don Mills, Ontario M3C 3N1

Macmillan Publishing Company is part of
the Maxwell Communication
Group of Companies.

First edition

Printed in Italy

10   9   8   7   6   5   4   3   2   1

ISBN 0-689-31863-4

CONTENTS

DRAMATIS PERSONÆ

(As arranged before commencement of game.)

	WHITE			RED	
PIECES	PAWNS		PAWNS		PIECES
Tweedledee	Daisy		Daisy		Humpty Dumpty
Unicorn	Haigha		Messenger		Carpenter
Sheep	Oyster		Oyster		Walrus
W. Queen	"Lily"		Tiger-lily		R. Queen
W. King	Fawn		Rose		R. King
Aged man	Oyster		Oyster		Crow
W. Knight	Hatta		Frog		R. Knight
Tweedledum....	Daisy		Daisy		Lion

A long, long time ago, when Lewis Carroll wrote this story, he worked out this chess problem, to show Alice's journey to become a Queen. If you can play chess, set out your pieces like this, and see if you can understand the clues, and follow Alice across the board. It is not like a real game, it is a Looking-glass game; something like a puzzle, and something like a map. I didn't find it easy. . . . Nohow.

T.R. 1992.

RED

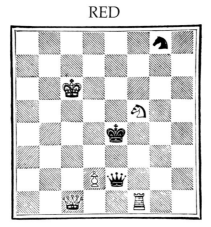

WHITE

White Pawn (Alice) to play and win in eleven moves.

Foreword

Everyone knows *Through the Looking- Glass* as a classic but it is also a very funny children's story. "I mean," as Tweedledum might say, "a funny story for children, *not* a story for funny children... nohow!" But how many of today's children actually read and understand the original?

As a little boy, although I liked it, it was the characters I liked, more than the text which I found difficult to follow and out of time and place. Returning to the book as an adult, I wanted to draw pictures of the characters, of Tweedledum and Tweedledee, of Humpty Dumpty and The Walrus and the Carpenter and I found it was the funny children's story that I wanted to illustrate. I realised that this meant simplifying Lewis Carroll's original text – an awesome task. Then I remembered that Lewis Carroll produced a nursery version of *Alice's Adventures in Wonderland* for very young children because "my ambition *now* is (is it a vain one?) to be read by children aged from nought to five. To be read? Nay, not so! Say rather to be thumbed, to be cooed over, to be dogs'-eared, to be rumpled, to be kissed, by the illiterate, ungrammatical, dimpled darlings, that fill your nursery with merry uproar and your inmost heart of hearts with a restful gladness!"

So I edited the text of *Through the Looking-Glass* by cutting some of the confusing bits and some of the outmoded bits. I have tried to reveal the story clearly but have kept very closely to Lewis Carroll's own words and more importantly his ideas.

And now, here is a book that is not an alternative to the original Tenniel/Carroll – which is available as a classic for all – but is a taste of the original for today's children. All the characters are here, all the poems are here and above all the humour is here. But most importantly, I hope that the spirit of the original masterpiece is here giving us the funny children's story that I first loved.

Tony Ross, Eastertide 1992

CHAPTER 1
Looking-glass House

One thing was certain, the white kitten had had nothing to do with it: it was the black kitten's fault entirely. For the white kitten had been having its face washed by the old cat, so you see, it *couldn't* have had any hand in the mischief.

But the black kitten had been finished with earlier, and so, while Alice was sitting curled up in the great armchair, half asleep, the kitten had been having a game with the ball of wool Alice had been trying to wind up, and there it was, all knots and tangles, with the kitten running after its own tail in the middle.

"Oh, you wicked little thing!" cried Alice, giving it a little kiss to make it understand it was in disgrace. "I was so angry, Kitty," she went on, "when I saw all the mischief you had been doing, I very nearly put you out into the snow! And you'd have deserved it, you little darling.

Now, I'm going to tell you all your faults. Number one: you squeaked twice while Dinah was washing your face this morning. You can't deny it, I heard you! What's that you say? Her paw went in your eye? Well, that's your fault for keeping your eyes open. Number two: you pulled Snowdrop away by the tail just as I had put down the saucer of milk before her! Number three: you unwound every bit of the wool while I wasn't looking!

"That's three faults, Kitty. I'm saving up all your punishments for Wednesday week – suppose they had saved up all my punishments!" she went on, more to herself than the kitten. "Suppose each punishment was to be going without a dinner; then I should have to go without fifty dinners at once. Well, I wouldn't mind *that*! I'd rather go without them than eat them!" Alice dropped the ball of wool. "Kitty, can you play chess? Don't smile, I'm asking it seriously. When we were playing just now, you watched as if you understood, and when I said 'Check!' you purred! Kitty dear – let's pretend – let's pretend we're kings and queens. Let's pretend that you're the Red Queen, Kitty. If you sat up and folded your arms, you'd look exactly like her."

And Alice got the Red Queen off the table, for the kitten to imitate; but it wouldn't fold its arms properly. So to punish it, she held it up to the looking-glass, that it might see how sulky it was. "And if you're not good directly," she added, "I'll put you *through* into Looking-glass House. Now, I'll tell you about Looking-glass House. First, the room you can see through the glass. That's the same as our drawing room, only the things go the other way. The books are like our books, only the words go the wrong way. I know *that* because I've held up one of our books to the glass, and then they hold one up in the other room.

"Now we come to the passage. It's very like our passage, only it may be *quite* different. Oh, Kitty, if only we could get through into Looking-glass House! Let's pretend there's a way! Let's pretend the glass has got soft like gauze. Why, it's turning into a sort of mist now . . ."

She was up on the chimney-piece, though she hardly knew how, and, certainly, the glass *was* beginning to melt away.

In another moment, Alice was through the glass and had jumped down into the Looking-glass room. She began looking about, and noticed that what could be seen from the

old room was quite uninteresting, but the rest was as different as possible. For instance, the pictures on the wall next to the fire seemed to be alive, and the clock on the chimney-piece (you can only see the back of it in the Looking-glass) had got the grinning face of a little old man.

Alice noticed several chessmen down in the hearth, and in a moment she was on her hands and knees watching them. They were walking about, two and two.

"Here are the Red King and the Red Queen," Alice said, "and there are the White King and the White Queen, sitting on the shovel – and there are two Castles, arm in arm. I don't think they can hear me and I'm sure they can't see me."

Something squeaked on the table, and Alice turned her head just in time to see one of the pawns roll over and begin kicking.

"It is the voice of my child!" the White Queen cried, as she rushed past the King, knocking him over among the cinders. "My precious Lily!"

"Fiddlesticks!" said the King, rubbing his nose, which had been hurt by the fall.

Alice was anxious to be of use, and she picked up the Queen and set her on the table by her noisy little daughter.

The Queen gasped and sat down. The rapid journey

through the air had taken her breath away and she could do nothing but hug little Lily. When she recovered her breath, she called to the White King, who was sitting in the ashes, "Mind the volcano!"

"What volcano?" said the King, looking anxiously into the fire.

"Blew – me – up!" panted the Queen. "You come the regular way. Don't get blown up."

Alice watched the King as he struggled from bar to bar, till at last she said, "You'll be hours getting to the table at that rate. I'll help you." It was clear that the King could neither hear nor see her, so Alice lifted him more slowly than she had lifted the Queen. The King made such a face when he

found himself held in the air by an invisible hand, his eyes and mouth went on getting larger and rounder, till Alice shook with laughter and put him on the table. He fell flat on his back, and lay perfectly still.

Alice was a little alarmed, and went to find water to throw over him. She could find nothing, and when she got back, the King had recovered and was talking to the Queen.

"The *horror* of the moment," he was saying, "I shall *never* forget."

"You will!" the Queen said. "If you don't make a note of it." The King took an enormous note-book, and began writing. A sudden thought struck Alice. She took hold of the end of the pencil, which came over his shoulder, and began writing for him.

The poor King looked unhappy and struggled with the pencil, but Alice was too strong for him. At last, he panted, "You know, dear, I must get a thinner pencil. I can't manage this one. It writes things I don't intend."

"What manner of things?" said the Queen, looking at the book (in which Alice had put *"The White Knight is falling off the poker"*).

There was a book near Alice, on the table, and while she watched the King, she turned its pages to find a part she could read. It was like this:

JABBERWOCKY

'Twas brillig, and the slithy toves
    Did gyre and gimble in the wabe:
All mimsy were the borogoves,
    And the mome raths outgrabe.

She puzzled over this for some time, then a bright thought struck her. "Why, it's a Looking-glass book! If I hold it up to a glass, the words will all go the right way again."

This was the poem that Alice read.

JABBERWOCKY

'Twas brillig, and the slithy toves
    Did gyre and gimble in the wabe:
All mimsy were the borogoves,
    And the mome raths outgrabe.

"Beware the Jabberwock, my son!
    The jaws that bite, the claws that catch!
Beware the Jubjub bird, and shun
    The frumious Bandersnatch!"

He took his vorpal sword in hand:
    Long time the manxome foe he sought —
So rested he by the Tumtum tree,
    And stood awhile in thought.

The jaws that bite, the claws that catch!

And, as in uffish thought he stood,
  The Jabberwock, with eyes of flame,
Came whiffling through the tulgey wood,
  And burbled as it came!

One, two! One, two! And through and through
  The vorpal blade went snicker-snack!
He left it dead, and with its head
  He went galumphing back.

"And hast thou slain the Jabberwock?
  Come to my arms, my beamish boy!
O frabjous day! Callooh! Callay!"
  He chortled in his joy.

'Twas brillig, and the slithy toves
  Did gyre and gimble in the wabe;
All mimsy were the borogoves,
  And the mome raths outgrabe.

"It seems very pretty," Alice said when she had finished it, "but it's rather hard to understand. But, oh, if I don't make haste, I shall have to go back through the Looking-glass before I've seen the rest of the house. Let's have a look at the garden!"

CHAPTER 2

The Garden of Live Flowers

"I should see the garden better," said Alice to herself, "if I could get to the top of that hill: and here's a path that leads straight to it. But how curiously it twists! It's more like a corkscrew than a path." She wandered up and down, trying turn after turn, but she always found herself back at the house.

"Oh, it's too bad!" she cried. "I never saw such a house for getting in the way!" However, there was the hill in sight, so she had to start again. This time she came upon a flower-bed, with a willow-tree in the middle.

"Oh, Tiger-lily," said Alice to one that was gracefully waving in the wind, "I *wish* you could talk!"

"We *can* talk," said the Tiger-lily, "when there's anybody worth talking to." Alice was astonished. She spoke again – almost in a whisper.

"Can *all* the flowers talk?"

"As well as *you* can," said the Tiger-lily.

"It isn't manners for us to begin," said the Rose, "and I was wondering when you'd speak! Said I to myself, 'Her face has got *some* sense in it, though it's not a clever one!'"

Alice didn't like being criticised, so *she* began asking questions. "Aren't you sometimes frightened at being planted here, with nobody to take care of you?"

"There's the tree in the middle," said the Rose.

"Oh, Tiger-lily," said Alice, "I wish you could talk!"

"But what could it do, if any danger came?" Alice asked.

"It could bark," said the Rose.

"It could say 'Bough-wough!' " cried a Daisy. "That's why its branches are called boughs!"

"Didn't you know *that*?" cried another Daisy, and they all began shouting together.

"*Silence!*" cried the Tiger-lily, trembling with excitement. "They know I can't get at them, or they wouldn't dare do it!"

Alice stooped down to the daisies and whispered, "If you don't hold your tongues, I'll pick you!" There was silence, and several of the pink daisies turned white.

"How is it you can all talk so nicely?" said Alice.

"Put your hand down and feel the ground," said the Tiger-lily. "Then you'll know why."

Alice did so. "It's very hard," she said. "But what's that got to do with it?"

"In most gardens," the Tiger-lily said, "they make the beds too soft – so that the flowers are always asleep."

"I never thought of that!" said Alice.

"It's my opinion you never think *at all*," the Rose said severely.

"Are there any more people in the garden besides me?" Alice said, choosing not to notice the Rose's last remark.

"There's one other flower in the garden that can move about like you," said the Rose.

"Is she like me?" Alice asked eagerly.

"Well, she has the same awkward shape as you," the Rose said, "but she's redder – and her petals are shorter. I dare say you'll see her soon."

"She's coming!" cried the Larkspur. "I hear her footstep, thump, thump."

Alice looked round eagerly, and found it was the Red Queen. "She's grown a good deal!" Alice remarked. She had indeed. When Alice first found her, she had been only three inches high – and here she was, taller than Alice herself.

"It's the fresh air that does it," said the Rose.

"I think I'll go and meet her," said Alice.

"To do that I should advise you to walk the other way," said the Rose.

This sounded nonsense to Alice so she set off at once towards the Red Queen. To her surprise, she lost sight of her in a moment and found herself at the house again. So, a little provoked, she thought she *would* try walking in the opposite direction, and soon found herself facing the Red Queen.

"Where did you come from?" said the Red Queen. "And where are you going? Look up, speak nicely and don't twiddle your fingers!"

Alice explained that she had lost her way.

"I don't know what you mean by *your* way," said the Queen. "All the ways about here belong to *me* — but why did you come here at all?" she added in a kinder tone. "Curtsey while you're thinking what to say, it saves time. And always say 'your Majesty'."

"I only wanted to see the garden, your Majesty —"

"That's right," said the Queen, patting her on the head, "though when you said 'garden', I've seen gardens, compared with which this would be a wilderness."

Alice went on, " — and I thought I'd try to find my way to the top of that hill —"

"When you say 'hill'," the Queen interrupted, "I could show you hills in comparison with which you'd call that a valley."

"No, I shouldn't," said Alice. "A hill *can't* be a valley. That would be nonsense."

Alice curtseyed again, afraid that the Queen was a little offended, and they walked on in silence to the top of the little hill. For some minutes Alice stood, looking over the country. There were a number of little brooks running across from side to side, and the ground between was divided into squares by a number of hedges.

"It's marked out just like a large chessboard!" Alice said at last. "There ought to be some men moving about somewhere — and so there are! It's a great game of chess that's being played — all over the world. Oh, what fun! How I wish that I might join in! I should love to be a Queen."

She glanced shyly at the real Queen, who smiled and said, "You can be the White Queen's Pawn, if you like; and you're in the Second Square to begin with. When you get into the Eighth Square, you'll be a Queen."

Just at this moment, somehow they began to run, hand in hand. The Queen kept crying "Faster!" but Alice felt that she could not go faster, though she had no breath to say so. The most curious thing was that the things around them never changed their places at all: however fast they went, they never seemed to pass anything. The Queen cried "Faster! Faster!" until they seemed to skim the air.

Suddenly, just as Alice was getting quite exhausted, they stopped and she found herself sitting on the ground, breathless and giddy. "Why, I do believe we've been under this tree all the time!" she said. "Everything's just as it was!"

"Of course it is," said the Queen.

"In *our* country," panted Alice, "you'd get to somewhere else, if you ran very fast for a long time."

"I'll take the measurements."

"A slow sort of country!" said the Queen. "Now, *here*, you see, it takes all the running you can do, to keep in the same place. If you want to get somewhere else, you must run twice as fast!"

"I'd rather not try," said Alice. "I'm so hot and thirsty."

"I know what you'd like!" the Queen said, taking a little box out of her pocket. "Have a biscuit!"

Alice took it, and ate it. It was so dry, she nearly choked.

"While you're refreshing yourself," said the Queen, "I'll take the measurements." And she took a ribbon out of her pocket, marked in inches, and began measuring out the ground and sticking little pegs in it. "At the end of *two* yards," she said, putting in a peg to mark the distance, "I shall give you your directions. At the end of *three* yards I shall repeat them. At the end of *four* I shall say good-bye, and at the end of *five*, I shall go!"

She had got all the pegs in by this time, and Alice looked on with great interest.

At the two-yard peg she said, "A pawn goes two squares in its first move. So you'll go very quickly through the Third Square, by railway, and you'll find yourself in the Fourth Square. *That* belongs to Tweedledum and Tweedledee. The Fifth is mostly water. The Sixth belongs to Humpty Dumpty. The Seventh Square is all forest – one of the Knights will show you the way – and in the Eighth Square, we shall be Queens together."

Alice got up and curtseyed, and sat down again.

At the next peg the Queen said, "Speak in French when you can't think of the English for a thing, turn out your toes as you walk, and remember who you are." She walked on quickly to the next peg, where she turned to say "good-bye", and then hurried to the last, and then she was gone.

Alice remembered she was a Pawn and began her move.

CHAPTER 3

Looking-glass Insects

The first thing to do was to make a survey of the country she was going to travel through.

"Principal rivers – there are none. Principal mountains – I'm on the only one. Principal towns – why, what *are* those creatures making honey down there? They can't be bees. Nobody ever saw bees a mile off." She stood watching one of them, bustling about among the flowers. This was anything but a regular bee; in fact, it was an elephant.

"And what enormous flowers they must be!" she thought. "Something like cottages with the roofs taken off. I'll go down and – no, I won't, not without a good long branch to brush them away."

"I think I'll go down the other way," she said after a pause, "and perhaps I may visit the elephants later. I do so want to get into the Third Square!" So, she ran down the hill and jumped over the first of the six little brooks.

"Tickets, please!" said the Guard, putting his head in at the window. In a moment, everybody in the carriage was holding out a ticket. "Now then, show your ticket, child!" the Guard went on, looking angrily at Alice.

In fact, it was an elephant.

A great many voices all said together, "Don't keep him waiting, child! Why, his time is worth a thousand pounds a minute."

"I'm afraid I haven't got one," said Alice. "There wasn't a ticket-office where I came from."

"Don't make excuses," said the Guard, "you should have bought one from the engine-driver."

And the chorus of voices went on, "Why, the smoke alone is worth a thousand pounds a puff!"

"I shall dream about a thousand pounds tonight!" thought Alice.

All this time the Guard was looking at her through a telescope, then a microscope, then an opera-glass. At last he said, "You're travelling the wrong way," and went away.

"A child," said the gentleman sitting opposite her (he was dressed in white paper) "ought to know where she is going, even if she doesn't know her own name."

A Goat, sitting next to the gentleman, said, "She ought to

know her way to the ticket-office, even if she doesn't know the alphabet."

The Beetle sitting next to the Goat, said, "She'll have to go back from here as luggage!"

Alice couldn't see who spoke next, but a hoarse voice said, "Change engines!"

"It sounds like a horse," Alice thought. And a very small voice next to her ear said,

"You might make a joke on that, you know, 'horse' and 'hoarse'."

The gentleman in white paper whispered, "Never mind what they say, my dear."

"I shan't," said Alice. "I don't belong here at all. I was in a wood just now, and I wish I could get back there."

"You might make a joke on that,"

 said the little voice,

"something about 'would' and 'could', you know."

Alice looked in vain for the voice. It sounded so unhappy.

"I know you're a friend,"

 it went on,

"and you won't hurt me, though I am an insect."

"What kind of insect?" Alice asked, anxious to know whether it could sting or not.

"What, you don't"

the little voice began, when there came a scream from the engine, and everybody jumped up in alarm.

In her fright, she took hold of the nearest thing.

"It's only a brook we have to jump over," said another voice quietly.

Alice felt nervous at the idea of trains jumping. "However, it'll take us into the Fourth Square," she thought. In her fright, she took hold of the nearest thing, which was the Goat's beard, as the carriage rose up into the air.

But the beard seemed to melt away and Alice found herself sitting under a tree, with the Gnat (the insect she had been talking to) balanced on a twig overhead. It was a *large* Gnat, about the size of a chicken.

"What, you don't like all insects?" the Gnat went on as if nothing had happened.

"I like them when they can talk. They don't where I come from," Alice said.

"What insects do you rejoice in where you come from?" the Gnat asked.

"I don't *rejoice* in them," said Alice. "But I know their names."

"In the wood down there, they've got no names," said the Gnat, "but go on."

"Well, there's the Horse-fly," Alice began.

"Right," said the Gnat, "halfway up that bush you'll see a Rocking-horse-fly. It's made of wood, and it gets about by swinging from branch to branch."

Alice looked at the Rocking-horse-fly with great interest. It looked bright, as if newly painted. She went on with her list. "There's the Dragon-fly . . ."

"On the branch above your head, there is a Snap-dragon-fly. Its body is a plum-pudding, its wings are holly leaves, and its head is a raisin burning in brandy. It nests in a Christmas box."

"Then there's the Butter-fly," Alice went on.

"Crawling at your feet," said the Gnat, "you may observe a Bread-and-butter-fly. Its wings are thin slices of bread and butter, its body is a crust, and its head a lump of sugar."

"What does it live on?" asked Alice.

"Weak tea with cream in it." The Gnat amused itself by humming around her head, then it settled again, and remarked, "I suppose you don't want to lose your name?"

"No, indeed!" Alice said.

"Only think how convenient it would be if you did," the Gnat went on. "For instance, if the teacher wanted to call you, she would call out 'Come here', and there she would have to leave off, because there would be no name."

"If she couldn't remember my name, she would call me 'Miss'," said Alice.

"If she said 'Miss', then you could miss your lessons," said the Gnat. "That's a joke, but a very bad one," and two tears rolled down his cheeks.

"You shouldn't make jokes, if it makes you unhappy," said Alice. With that the Gnat seemed to fade away before her eyes, so she got up and walked on.

Soon, she came to a field, with a wood on the other side of it. "This must be the wood where things have no names," she thought. "I wonder what will happen to my name when

I go in?" The wood was cool and shady. "It's a great comfort," said Alice, "after being so hot, to get into the . . . into the *what*?" She couldn't think of the word. "I mean . . . to get under . . . this . . ." She touched the tree. "Why, I do believe it's got no name." She thought for a minute. "And now, *who am I*?"

Just then, a Fawn came wandering by and looked at Alice with large, gentle eyes. "What do you call yourself?" the Fawn said, in a soft, sweet voice.

"I wish I knew!" thought Alice sadly. "Nothing, just now," she said. "Please tell me what you call yourself."

"I'll tell you if you'll come a little further on," said the Fawn. "I can't remember here."

They walked on together, Alice's arms clasped round the Fawn's neck, till they came to another open field. The Fawn shook itself free from Alice's arms, and cried out, "I'm a Fawn! And, dear me, you're a human child." A look of alarm came into its eyes, and it darted away at full speed.

Alice looked sadly after it. "At least, I know what I am now," she said. "Now, which of these finger-posts ought I to follow?" It was not a difficult question, as there was only one road, and the finger-posts both pointed along it, one marked "TO TWEEDLEDUM'S HOUSE" and the other "TO THE HOUSE OF TWEEDLEDEE".

"I do believe," said Alice at last, "that they live in the same house! I'll just call and say 'How d'you do?' and ask them the way out of the wood. If I could only get to the Eighth Square before·it gets dark!"

CHAPTER 4

Tweedledum and Tweedledee

They were standing under a tree, each with an arm round the other's neck. One of them had "DUM" embroidered on his collar, and the other "DEE". They stood so still that Alice quite forgot they were alive and, just as she was looking to see if "TWEEDLE" was written on the back of each collar, she was startled by a voice coming from the one marked "DUM".

"If you think we're wax-works," he said, "you ought to pay, you know. Wax-works weren't made to be looked at for nothing. Nohow!"

"Contrariwise," added the one marked "DEE", "if you think we're alive, you ought to speak."

"I'm sorry," said Alice, thinking of the words of the old song:

> *Tweedledum and Tweedledee*
>   *Agreed to have a battle;*
> *For Tweedledum said Tweedledee*
>   *Had spoiled his nice new rattle.*
>
> *Just then flew down a monstrous crow,*
>   *As black as a tar-barrel;*
> *Which frightened both the heroes so,*
>   *They quite forgot their quarrel.*

"I know what you're thinking about!" said Tweedledum.

They stood so still that Alice quite forgot they were alive.

"Contrariwise . . ." began Tweedledee.

"I was thinking," Alice said politely, "which is the way out of this wood: it's getting so dark." The little men grinned. They looked so like a couple of schoolboys that Alice pointed her finger at Tweedledum and said, "First boy!"

"Nohow!" Tweedledum cried, and shut his mouth with a snap.

"Next boy!" said Alice.

"Contrariwise!" shouted Tweedledee.

"You've begun wrong. The first thing in a visit," said Tweedledum, "is to say 'How d'you do?' and shake hands." They held out their two free hands. Alice took both hands at once, and the next moment, they were dancing round in a ring. The two fat dancers were soon out of breath, and they left off as suddenly as they had begun.

"I hope you're not too tired?" said Alice.

"Nohow, and thank you for asking," said Tweedledum.

"Much obliged," said Tweedledee. "You like poetry?"

"Ye–es," said Alice. "Would you tell me which road leads out of the wood?"

"What shall I repeat to her?" said Tweedledee, not noticing Alice's question.

"The *Walrus and the Carpenter* is the longest," said Tweedledum. Tweedledee began instantly:

"The sun was shining"

Here, Alice ventured to interrupt. "Would you please tell me first, which road?"

Tweedledee smiled gently, and began again:

> *"The sun was shining on the sea,*
>   *Shining with all his might:*
> *He did his very best to make*
>   *The billows smooth and bright –*
> *And this was odd, because it was*
>   *The middle of the night.*
>
> *The moon was shining sulkily,*
>   *Because she thought the sun*
> *Had got no business to be there*
>   *After the day was done —*
> *'It's very rude of him,' she said,*
>   *'To come and spoil the fun!'*

The sea was wet as wet could be,
The sands were dry as dry.
You could not see a cloud, because
No cloud was in the sky.
No birds were flying overhead—
There were no birds to fly.

The Walrus and the Carpenter
Were walking close at hand.
They wept like anything to see
Such quantities of sand.
'If this were only cleared away,'
They said, 'it **would** *be grand!'*

'If seven maids with seven mops
Swept it for half a year,
Do you suppose,' the Walrus said,
'That they could get it clear?'
'I doubt it,' said the Carpenter,
And shed a bitter tear.

'O Oysters, come and walk with us!'
The Walrus did beseech.
'A pleasant walk, a pleasant talk,
Along the briny beach:
We cannot do with more than four,
To give a hand to each.'

The eldest Oyster looked at him,
But never a word he said:
The eldest Oyster winked his eye,
And shook his heavy head—
Meaning to say he did not choose
To leave the oyster-bed.

'A pleasant walk, a pleasant talk, along the briny beach.'

But four young Oysters hurried up,
    All eager for the treat:
Their coats were brushed, their faces washed,
    Their shoes were clean and neat—
And this was odd, because, you know,
    They hadn't any feet.

Four other Oysters followed them,
    And yet another four;
And thick and fast they came at last,
    And more, and more, and more—
All hopping through the frothy waves,
    And scrambling to the shore.

The Walrus and the Carpenter
    Walked on a mile or so,
And then they rested on a rock,
    Conveniently low:
And all the little Oysters stood
    And waited in a row.

'The time has come,' the Walrus said,
    'To talk of many things:
Of shoes—and ships—and sealing-wax—
    Of cabbages—and kings—
And why the sea is boiling hot—
    And whether pigs have wings.'

'But wait a bit,' the Oysters cried,
    'Before we have our chat;
For some of us are out of breath,
    And all of us are fat!'
'No hurry!' said the Carpenter.
    They thanked him much for that.

And all the little Oysters stood and waited in a row.

'A loaf of bread,' the Walrus said,
  'Is what we chiefly need.
Pepper and vinegar besides
  Are very good indeed—
Now, if you're ready, Oysters dear,
  We can begin to feed.'

'But not on us!' the Oysters cried,
  Turning a little blue.
'After such kindness, that would be
  A dismal thing to do!'
'The night is fine,' the Walrus said.
  'Do you admire the view?

'It was so kind of you to come!
  And you are very nice!'
The Carpenter said nothing but
  'Cut us another slice.
I wish you were not quite so deaf—
  I've had to ask you twice!'

'It seems a shame,' the Walrus said,
   'To play them such a trick,
After we've brought them out so far,
   And made them trot so quick!'
The Carpenter said nothing but
   'The butter's spread too thick!'

'I weep for you,' the Walrus said,
   'I deeply sympathise.'
With sobs and tears he sorted out
   Those of the largest size,
Holding his pocket-handkerchief
   Before his streaming eyes.

'O Oysters,' said the Carpenter,
   'You've had a pleasant run!
Shall we be trotting home again?'
   But answer came there none—
And this was scarcely odd, because
   They'd eaten every one."

"I like the Walrus best," said Alice, "because he was a *little* sorry for the poor oysters."

"He ate more than the Carpenter, though," said Tweedledee.

"Then," Alice said indignantly, "I like the Carpenter best."

"But he ate as many as he could get," said Tweedledum.

Alice began, "Well! They were both very unpleasant–" Here she checked herself, in some alarm, hearing something that sounded like the puffing of a steam engine, though she feared it was more likely a wild beast.

"It's only the Red King snoring," said Tweedledee. "Come and look at him!" The brothers each took one of Alice's hands, and led her to where the King was sleeping. He wore a tall red nightcap and was lying crumpled in a sort of untidy heap.

"I'm afraid he'll catch cold lying on the damp grass," said Alice, thoughtfully.

"What do you think he's dreaming about?" said Tweedledee.

"Nobody can guess that," Alice said.

"Why, about *you*!" Tweedledee exclaimed. "And if he stopped dreaming about you, where do you suppose you'd be?"

"Where I am now, of course," said Alice.

"You'd go out – bang – just like a candle!" cried Tweedledum.

"I shouldn't," said Alice. "Anyway, *hush*! You'll be waking him."

"No use *your* talking about waking him," said Tweedledum. "You're only one of the things in his dream."

"I'm *real*!" said Alice, and began to cry. "If I wasn't real, I shouldn't be able to cry. I know they're talking nonsense," she thought, brushing away her tears. "Anyway, it's getting very dark. Do you think it's going to rain?"

Tweedledum spread a large umbrella over himself and his brother. "Not under here," he said. "Nohow!"

"Selfish things!" thought Alice, and she was just about to leave them, when Tweedledum sprang out from under the umbrella, yellow eyes bulging, and pointed a trembling finger at a small white thing lying under a tree.

"It's only an old rattle," said Alice, examining the little thing.

"It isn't old!" Tweedledum raged, looking at Tweedledee, who was trying to hide under the umbrella. "It's *new* – I bought it yesterday – my nice *new* rattle." His voice rose to a scream.

All this time, Tweedledee was trying to fold up the umbrella, but only succeeded in bundling himself up in it. He lay there, with his head sticking out, opening and shutting his mouth and large eyes. "He looks just like a fish," thought Alice.

"Of course you agree to have a battle?" Tweedledum said.

"I suppose so," the other sulkily replied, as he crawled out of the umbrella. "Only, she must help us dress up." The two brothers went off hand in hand, and returned with their arms full of bolsters, blankets, rugs, tablecloths, coal-scuttles, and pots and pans.

The *trouble* they gave Alice, tying strings and fastening buttons. "They'll be just like bundles of old clothes!" she thought, arranging a bolster around Tweedledee's neck, "to stop his head being cut off," as he said. Alice laughed aloud, but managed to change it into a cough.

"I'm usually quite brave, but today I happen to have a headache," said Tweedledum.

"And *I've* got a toothache!" cried Tweedledee quickly. "I'm far worse than you!"

"Then you'd better not fight today," said Alice.

"We must have a *bit* of a fight," said Tweedledum. "Let's fight till six, and then have dinner."

"Very well," said the other sadly. "And she can watch – only better not come too close. I hit everything in reach, whether I can see it or not."

"You must hit trees pretty often," Alice said with a laugh.

"There won't be a tree left round us by the time we've finished," said Tweedledum with a satisfied smile.

"And all about a rattle," said Alice.

"What a thick black cloud that is!"

"A *new* rattle!" said Tweedledum. "But we must begin quick. It's getting as dark as it can."

It was getting dark so suddenly that Alice thought there must be a thunderstorm coming on. "What a thick black cloud that is!" she said. "And how fast it comes! Why, I do believe it's got wings!"

"It's the crow!" Tweedledum cried in a shrill voice of alarm, and the two brothers took to their heels.

Alice ran into the wood, and stopped under a tree.

"I do wish it wouldn't flap its wings so," she thought. "It makes quite a hurricane. Here's someone's shawl being blown away!"

Alice caught the shawl and looked about for the owner.

CHAPTER 5

Wool and Water

Alice caught the shawl, and looked about for the owner. The White Queen came running wildly through the wood, arms stretched out as if flying. Alice went to meet her with the shawl, and helped her to put it on again.

"Am I addressing the White Queen?" she began timidly.

"Yes, if you call that a-dressing," said the Queen.

Alice didn't want to argue, so she smiled and said, "If your Majesty will tell me the right way to begin, I'll do it as well as I can."

"I don't want it to be done at all!" the poor Queen groaned. "I've been a-dressing myself for the last two hours."

"She's so dreadfully untidy!" thought Alice. "Everything's crooked and she's all over pins."

"May I put your shawl straight?" she asked aloud.

"I don't know what's the matter with it," the Queen said sadly. "I've pinned it, but there's no pleasing it!"

"It can't go straight, if you pin it all on one side," Alice said, as she put it right for her. "But really you should have a lady's maid!"

"I'll take *you*," said the Queen. "Twopence a week, and jam every other day."

Alice laughed. "I don't want you to hire me and I don't like jam!"

"You couldn't have it if you *did* want it," the Queen said.

"The rule is, jam yesterday and jam tomorrow – but never jam today."

"It must come sometimes to 'jam today'," Alice objected.

"No!" said the Queen. "Jam every *other* day. Today isn't any *other* day, you know!"

"I'm confused," said Alice.

"That's the effect of living backwards," the Queen said kindly. "It makes one giddy."

"Living backwards! I never heard of such a thing!" said Alice, astonished.

"For instance," the Queen went on, sticking a large piece of plaster on her finger, "take the King's Messenger. He's in prison now, and the trial doesn't even begin till next Wednesday – and, of course, the crime comes last of all."

"Suppose he never commits the crime?" said Alice.

"That would be all the better, wouldn't it?" the Queen said, as she bound the plaster round her finger with a bit of ribbon.

Alice was just beginning to say, "There's a mistake there somewhere . . ." when the Queen began screaming, "My finger's bleeding! Oh, oh, oh, oh!"

"What *is* the matter?" said Alice. "Have you pricked your finger?"

"Not yet," the Queen said.

"When do you expect to do it?" Alice asked, close to laughter.

"When I fasten my shawl again," the poor Queen groaned. Just then, she clutched wildly at her shawl.

"Take care!" cried Alice, but it was too late. The pin had slipped, and the Queen had pricked her finger.

"That accounts for the bleeding," said the Queen with a smile.

"But why don't you scream *now*?" said Alice.

"Why, I've done the screaming already," said the Queen.

By this time it was getting light. "The crow must have flown away, I think," said Alice.

The pin had come undone again, and a sudden gust of wind blew the shawl across a little brook. The Queen spread her arms again and went flying after it, this time catching it for herself. "I've got it!" she cried. "Now I will pin it on all by myself."

"Then I hope your finger is better?" said Alice politely, as she crossed the little brook after the Queen.

"Oh, *much* better," said the Queen, her voice rising into a squeak. "Much be-etter! Be-e-e-tter! Be-e-ehh!" The last word ended in a bleat, like a sheep. Alice looked at the Queen, who seemed to have suddenly wrapped herself in wool. Was she in a shop? Was that really a *sheep* sitting behind the counter?

She was in a little dark shop and opposite her was an old Sheep sitting in an arm-chair, knitting.

"What is it you want to buy?" the Sheep said.

"I don't quite know yet," said Alice. "I'd like to look all round first."

"You may look in front of you, and on both sides," said the Sheep, "but you can't look *all* round you, unless you've got eyes at the back of your head."

The shop was full of curious things, but the odd thing was that whenever Alice looked hard at any shelf, it was always quite empty, though all the others round it were full.

The Sheep took up another pair of needles. She was working with fourteen pairs at once and Alice looked at her in great astonishment. "Can you row?" the Sheep asked, handing her a pair of knitting needles as she spoke.

"Can you row?" the sheep asked.

"Yes, but not on land, and not with needles . . ." Alice began, when suddenly the needles turned into oars in her hands and she found they were in a little boat, gliding along between banks.

"Feather!" cried the Sheep, as she took up another pair of needles.

Alice pulled away without a reply. There was something very queer about the water, she thought, as every now and then the oars got stuck fast in it and would hardly come out again.

"Didn't you hear me say 'Feather'?" the Sheep cried angrily, taking up more needles.

"Indeed I did," said Alice. "But *why*? I'm not a bird!"

"You are," said the Sheep. "You're a little goose."

This offended Alice, and there was no more conversation for a minute or two. The boat glided on, sometimes among beds of weeds, sometimes under trees, always with the same riverbanks frowning overhead.

"Oh, please!" Alice cried suddenly. "There are some scented rushes and they're such beauties!"

"You needn't say 'please' to *me* about 'em," said the Sheep, without looking up from her knitting. "I didn't put 'em there!"

"I meant – please, may we pick some?" Alice pleaded. "If you don't mind stopping the boat for a minute."

"How am *I* to stop it?" said the Sheep. "If you leave off rowing, it'll stop of itself." So the boat was left to drift, till it glided gently among the waving rushes.

Alice rolled up her sleeves and plunged her arms into the water to get hold of the rushes a good long way down before breaking them off. She forgot all about the Sheep and the knitting as she bent over the side of the boat, with the ends of her hair dipping into the water. "I hope the boat won't tipple over!" she said to herself. "Oh, what a lovely one, I

"I hope the boat won't tipple over!" she said to herself.

just can't reach it. The prettiest are always out of reach." She scrambled back to her place in the boat and began to arrange her new treasures.

Just then, the rushes began to fade. Even real scented rushes last only a very little while and these dream-rushes melted away like snow. But Alice hardly noticed. There were so many other curious things to think about. Suddenly one of the oars got fast in the water, and *wouldn't* come out. The handle of it caught Alice under the chin and swept her off her seat, into the heap of rushes.

The Sheep went on knitting, as if nothing had happened. "That was a nice crab you caught!" she remarked.

"Was it? I would have liked a little crab to take home with me," said Alice, peeping into the dark water. "Are there many here?"

The Sheep laughed full of scorn, "Crabs and all sorts of things. What *do* you want to buy?"

"To *buy*?" Alice echoed in astonishment, for the river had vanished and she was back in the little shop.

"I would like an egg, please," she said timidly.

"Fivepence for one, twopence for two," the Sheep replied.

"Then two are cheaper than one?" Alice said, in a surprised tone.

"Only, you must eat them both if you buy two," said the Sheep.

"Then I'll have one, please," said Alice.

The Sheep took her money, then said, "I never put things into people's hands, you must get it for yourself." And so saying, she went to the other end of the shop, and set the egg upright on a shelf.

Alice groped her way among the tables and chairs, for the shop was dark towards the end. "The egg seems further away, the more I walk towards it. Let me see, is this a chair? Why, it's got branches! How odd to find trees here! And actually here's a little brook . . ."

So she went on. As everything turned into a tree the moment she came up to it, she quite expected the egg to do the same.

CHAPTER 6
Humpty Dumpty

However, the egg only got larger and larger, and more and more human: when she came within a few yards of it, she saw that it had eyes and a nose and mouth; and when she came close to it, she saw clearly that it was Humpty Dumpty himself. He was sitting with his legs crossed, on top of a high wall.

"How like an egg he looks!" said Alice, standing with her hands ready to catch him, for she was every moment expecting him to fall.

"It's *very* provoking," said Humpty Dumpty, after a long silence, "to be called an egg!"

"I said you *looked* like an egg, sir," Alice explained. "Some eggs are very pretty, you know."

"Some people have no more sense than a baby," replied Humpty Dumpty.

Alice did not know what to say to this, so she stood and softly repeated to herself:

> *"Humpty Dumpty sat on a wall:*
> *Humpty Dumpty had a great fall.*
> *All the King's horses and all the King's men*
> *Couldn't put Humpty Dumpty in his place again."*

"Don't stand chattering to yourself," Humpty Dumpty said. "Tell me your name and business."

"How like an egg he looks," said Alice.

"My *name* is Alice, but –"

"It's a stupid enough name!" Humpty Dumpty interrupted. "What does it mean?"

"Must a name *mean* something?" Alice asked doubtfully.

"Of course!" Humpty Dumpty said with a short laugh. "*My* name means the shape I am. With a name like yours, you might be any shape."

"Why do you sit here all alone?" Alice said, not wishing to argue.

"Why, because there's nobody with me," cried Humpty Dumpty.

"Don't you think you'd be safer down on the ground?" Alice went on.

"Of course I don't think so!" Humpty Dumpty growled. "Why, if ever I did fall, which there's no chance of, but if I did . . ." (he looked so solemn that Alice nearly laughed) " . . . why, the King has promised, with his own mouth, to . . . to . . ."

"To send all his horses and all his men," Alice interrupted.

"Now I declare that's too bad!" Humpty Dumpty cried angrily. "You've been listening at doors, and down chimneys, or you couldn't have known it!"

"I haven't," Alice said gently. "It's in a book."

"Ah, well," Humpty Dumpty said in a calmer tone. "If it's in a book, that's what you call history, that is. Now, look at me. *I've* spoken to a King, and to show you I'm not proud, you may shake hands with me!" Grinning from ear to ear, he leaned forwards (and nearly fell off the wall doing it) and offered Alice his hand. Anxiously, she took it.

"If he smiles much more, the ends of his mouth will meet behind and the top of his head will fall off!" she thought.

"Yes, all his horses and all his men," Humpty Dumpty went on. "However, let's get back to the last remark but one."

"I'm afraid I can't remember it," said Alice politely.

"In that case, we'll start afresh," said Humpty Dumpty. "How old did you say you were?"

"Seven years and six months," said Alice.

"Wrong!" Humpty Dumpty exclaimed. "You never said a word about it."

"I thought you meant, 'How old *are* you?'" Alice explained.

"If I'd meant that, I'd have said it," said Humpty Dumpty.

Alice did not want another argument, so she said, "What a lovely belt you've got on! At least, a beautiful cravat, I should have said . . . no, belt . . ." Humpty Dumpty looked offended, and Alice went on, " . . . I mean, oh, dear, if only I knew what was neck and what was waist."

Humpty Dumpty said nothing for a minute or two. When he did speak again, it was in an angry growl. "It's a cravat, child, and a beautiful one, as you say. A present from the White King and Queen." He crossed one knee over the other. "They gave it to me for an un-birthday present."

"I beg your pardon?" Alice said. "What is an *un*-birthday present?"

"A present given when it's not your birthday, of course."

Alice considered this. "I prefer birthday presents," she said.

"You don't know what you're talking about," cried Humpty Dumpty. "How many days are there in a year?"

"Three hundred and sixty-five," said Alice.

"And how many birthdays have you?"

"One."

"And if you take one from three hundred and sixty-five, what remains?"

"Three hundred and sixty-four, of course."

Humpty Dumpty looked doubtful. "I'd rather see that done on paper," he said.

Alice smiled as she took out her note-book, and worked the sum for him:

Humpty Dumpty took the book, and looked at it. "That *seems* to be right –" he began.

"You're holding it upside down!" Alice interrupted.

"To be sure I was!" Humpty Dumpty laughed. "I thought it looked queer. It shows three hundred and sixty-four days when you might get *un*-birthday presents and only one for birthday presents. There's glory for you!"

"I don't know what you mean by 'glory'," Alice said.

Humpty Dumpty smiled. "Of course you don't – till I tell you. It means 'there's a nice argument for you!'"

"'Glory' doesn't mean 'a nice argument'," Alice objected.

"When *I* use a word, it means whatever I choose it to mean," said Humpty Dumpty scornfully. "And what I really meant by 'glory' was that we've had enough of that subject, and it would be just as well if you'd say what you mean to do next, as I suppose you don't intend to stop here all your life."

"That's a lot for one word to mean," Alice said thoughtfully. "But, as you seem very clever at explaining words, sir, would you tell me the meaning of the poem *Jabberwocky*?"

"Let's hear it," said Humpty Dumpty. "I can explain all the poems ever invented – and a good many that haven't been invented just yet."

This sounded hopeful, so Alice started the first verse:

> *" 'Twas brillig, and the slithy toves*
> *Did gyre and gimble in the wabe:*
> *All mimsy were the borogoves,*
> *All the mome raths outgrabe."*

"That's enough," Humpty Dumpty interrupted, "there are plenty of hard words there. '*Brillig*' means four o'clock in the afternoon, the time when you *broil* things for dinner. '*Slithy*' means 'lithe and slimy' – there are two meanings packed into one word."

"I see," Alice remarked thoughtfully, "and what are '*toves*'?"

"Well, '*toves*' are something like badgers, they're something like lizards, and they're something like corkscrews."

"They must be very curious creatures," said Alice.

"They are that," said Humpty Dumpty. "They make their nests under sundials, and live on cheese."

"And what's to '*gyre*' and '*gimble*'?"

"'*Gyre*' is to go round like a gyroscope, and '*gimble*' is to make holes like a gimlet."

"And the '*wabe*' is the grass around the sundial, I suppose?" said Alice.

"Exactly so. *'Mimsy'* is 'flimsy and miserable' and *'borogove'* is a shabby-looking bird with feathers sticking out like a live mop."

"And *'mome raths'*?" said Alice.

"Well, a *'rath'* is a sort of green pig, but I'm not certain about *'mome'*. I think it's short for 'from home', you know, lost."

"And what does *'outgrabe'* mean?"

"Well, *'outgribing'* is something between bellowing and whistling, with a sneeze in the middle. Who's been repeating all this hard stuff to you?"

"I read it in a book," said Alice.

"*I* can repeat poetry," said Humpty Dumpty.

"Oh, you needn't," Alice said hastily, hoping to stop him.

"This piece was written entirely for you," he went on.

Alice felt that in that case, she really ought to listen, so she sat down and said, "Thank you."

"In winter, when the fields are white,
I sing this song for your delight –

only I don't sing it," he explained.

"I see you don't," said Alice.

"In spring, when woods are getting green,
I'll try and tell you what I mean."

"Thank you very much," said Alice.

"In summer, when the days are long,
Perhaps you'll understand the song.

In autumn, when the leaves are brown,
Take pen and ink and write it down."

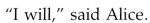

"I will," said Alice.

"You needn't go on making remarks like that," Humpty Dumpty said. "They are silly, and they put me off.

I sent a message to the fish:
I told them 'This is what I wish.'

The little fishes of the sea,
They sent an answer back to me.

The little fishes' answer was
'We cannot do it, sir, because . . .'

"I'm afraid I don't understand," said Alice.

"It gets easier further on," Humpty Dumpty replied.

"I sent to them again to say
'It will be better to obey.'

The fishes answered with a grin,
'Why, what a temper you are in!'

I told them once, I told them twice.
They would not listen to advice.

I took a kettle large and new
   Fit for the deed I had to do.

My heart went hop, my heart went thump.
   I filled the kettle at the pump.

Then someone came to me and said,
   'The little fishes are in bed.'

I said to him, I said it plain,
   'Then you must wake them up again.'

I said it very loud and clear
   I went and shouted in his ear.

But he was very stiff and proud.
   He said 'You needn't shout so loud!'

And he was very proud and stiff.
   He said 'I'd go and wake them if –'

I took a corkscrew from the shelf.
   I went to wake them up myself.

And when I found the door was locked,
   I pulled and pushed and kicked and knocked.

And when I found the door was shut,
   I tried to turn the handle, but –'

There was a long pause.

   "Is that all?" Alice timidly asked.

   "That's all," said Humpty Dumpty. "Good-bye."

   This was so sudden and such a very strong hint that Alice held out her hand. "Good-bye, till we meet again," she said cheerfully.

"I wouldn't know you if we did meet again," said Humpty Dumpty. "You're so exactly like other people. Now, if you had two eyes on the same side of the nose . . . or the mouth at the top . . ."

Alice waited to see if he would speak again, but he took no further notice of her, so she began to walk quietly away. Suddenly, a heavy crash shook the forest from end to end.

CHAPTER 7

The Lion and the Unicorn

The next moment, soldiers came running through the woods, at first in twos and threes, then in such crowds that Alice got behind a tree for fear of being run over.

She had never seen soldiers so uncertain on their feet: they were always tripping over. Whenever one went down, several more always fell over him, until the ground was covered with little heaps of men. The horses managed better, but whenever one stumbled, the rider fell off immediately. As the confusion got worse, Alice was glad to get into an open place, where she found the White King busily writing in his note-book.

"I've sent them all!" he cried, on seeing Alice. "Did you see any soldiers, my dear?"

"Yes," said Alice, "several thousand, I should think."

"Four thousand, two hundred and seven," the King said, referring to his book. I didn't send the two Messengers, though. They're both gone to town. Just look along the road and tell me if you can see them."

Alice shaded her eyes with one hand. "I can see somebody," she said, "but what curious attitudes he goes into." (The Messenger kept skipping up and down, and wriggling like an eel, with his great hands spread out like fans on each side.)

"He's an Anglo-Saxon Messenger," said the King, "and

She had never seen soldiers so uncertain on their feet.

those are Anglo-Saxon attitudes. His name is Haigha." (He pronounced it to rhyme with mayor.) "The other Messenger's called Hatta. I must have two, you know – one to come, and one to go; one to fetch and one to carry."

When the Messenger arrived, he was far too out of breath to say anything. He could only wave his hands about and make the most fearful faces at the poor King.

"You alarm me!" said the King. "I feel faint! Give me a ham sandwich."

The Messenger opened the bag hanging round his neck, and handed a sandwich to the King, who devoured it greedily.

"Another!" said the King.

"There's only hay left now," the Messenger said, peeping into the bag.

"Hay, then," the King murmured. "There's nothing like eating hay when you're faint."

"I should think throwing cold water over you would be better," Alice said.

"I didn't say there was nothing *better*," the King replied. "I said there was nothing *like* it. Tell us what is happening in the town," the King went on, holding out his hand for more hay.

"I'll whisper it," said the Messenger, stooping close to the King's ear. However, instead of whispering, he shouted at the top of his voice, "They're at it again!"

"Do you call that a whisper?" cried the poor King. "If you do that again, I'll have you buttered!"

"Who are at it again?" Alice asked.

"Why, the Lion and the Unicorn, fighting for the crown," said the King. "And the joke is, it's *my* crown all the while. Let's run and see them." And they trotted off, Alice repeating to herself the words of the old song:

> *"The Lion and the Unicorn were fighting for the crown,*
> *The Lion beat the Unicorn all round the town.*
> *Some gave them white bread and some gave them brown,*
> *Some gave them plum-cake and drummed them out of town."*

"And does . . . the one that wins . . . get the crown?" she gasped, as the long run had quite put her out of breath.

"Dear me, no!" said the King. "What an idea!"

Alice had no more breath for talking, so they trotted on in silence, till they came to where the Lion and the Unicorn were fighting. They were in such a cloud of dust that Alice could only distinguish the Unicorn by his horn. They placed themselves close to where Hatta, the other Messenger, was standing, with a cup of tea and a piece of bread and butter.

"Hatta's only just out of prison, and he hadn't finished his tea when he was sent in," Haigha whispered to Alice.

Hatta nodded, and went on with his bread and butter.

"Were you happy in prison, dear child?" Haigha asked. A tear trickled down Hatta's cheek, but not a word would he say.

"Speak, won't you?" cried the King. "How are they getting on with the fight?"

Hatta swallowed a large piece of bread and butter. "They're

getting on well. Each of them has been down about eighty-seven times," he said.

"Ten minutes for refreshments!" called the King, and the Lion and the Unicorn sat down, panting. Hatta and Haigha carried round trays of white and brown bread.

"I don't think they'll fight any more today," the King said to Hatta. "Go and order the drums to begin." Hatta bounded away like a grasshopper.

At this moment, the Unicorn sauntered by, with his hands in his pockets.

"I had the best of it this time," he said to the King.

"You shouldn't have run him through with your horn, you know," the King replied nervously.

"It didn't hurt him," the Unicorn replied, when his eye fell on Alice. He looked at her with an air of deep disgust. "What is *this*?" he said.

"It's a child," Haigha answered. "We found it today."

"I always thought they were fabulous monsters!" said the Unicorn. "Is it alive?"

"It can talk," said Haigha solemnly.

The Unicorn looked dreamily at Alice, and said, "Talk, child."

"It's a child," Haigha answered. "We found it today."

"I always thought *unicorns* were fabulous monsters, too," Alice said with a smile.

"Well, now we have seen each other," said the Unicorn. "If you will believe in me, I will believe in you."

"It's a bargain," said Alice.

"Come, fetch the plum-cake, old man!" the Unicorn went on, turning to the King. "None of your brown bread for me."

As Haigha took a large cake out of his bag, the Lion joined them. "What's this?" he growled, blinking sleepily at Alice. "Are you animal . . . or vegetable . . . or mineral?"

"It's a fabulous monster!" the Unicorn cried out, before Alice could reply.

"Then hand round the plum-cake, Monster," the Lion said. "And we'll all sit down." The King was uncomfortable, sitting between the two great creatures, but there was no other place for him.

"What a fight we might have for the crown *now*!" the Unicorn said, looking slyly at the crown. It was nearly falling off the King's head, he was trembling so much.

"I should win easily," said the Lion. "Why, I beat you all round the town, you chicken."

"Did you go by the old bridge, or the market place?" the King interrupted nervously, trying to prevent a quarrel.

"I'm sure I don't know," the Lion growled. "There was too much dust to see anything. What a time the Monster's taking, cutting up that cake!" Alice was sitting by a little brook, sawing away with a knife.

"You don't know how to manage Looking-glass cake," the Unicorn remarked. "Hand it round first and cut it afterwards."

This sounded nonsense, but Alice got up and carried the dish round, and the cake divided itself into three pieces.

"*Now* cut it up," the Lion said, as she sat down with the empty dish.

"I say, this isn't fair!" cried the Unicorn. "The Monster has given the Lion twice as much as me!"

But before Alice could answer him, the drums began. Where the noise came from, she couldn't make out, but it rang through her head till she felt quite deafened. In her terror she sprang across

the brook, just in time to see the Lion and the Unicorn rise to their feet. She put her hands to her ears, trying to shut out the dreadful uproar.

"If *that* doesn't 'drum them out of town'," she thought to herself, "nothing ever will!"

CHAPTER 8

"It's my own invention"

After a while the noise seemed to die away and Alice lifted her head. There was no one to be seen and her first thought was that she must have been dreaming about the Lion and the Unicorn.

Her thoughts were interrupted by a loud "Ahoy! Ahoy! Check!" and a Knight, dressed in crimson armour, came galloping down upon her. As he reached her, the horse stopped suddenly. "You're my prisoner!" the Knight cried, as he tumbled off.

Alice watched with some anxiety as he mounted again. As soon as he was comfortably in the saddle, he began once more, "You're my –" but here another voice broke in, "Ahoy! Ahoy! Check!" This time it was a White Knight. He drew up at Alice's side, and tumbled off his horse, just as the Red Knight had done. Then he got on again and the two Knights sat and looked at each other.

"She's *my* prisoner!" the Red Knight said at last.

"Yes, but then I rescued her!" the White Knight replied.

"Well, we must fight for her!" said the Red Knight, taking up his helmet (which was shaped something like a horse's head).

"You will observe the Rules of Battle, then?" the White Knight asked. They began banging away furiously.

"I wonder what the Rules of Battle are," Alice said to herself, hiding behind a tree. "One Rule seems to be that if one Knight hits the other, he knocks him off his horse, and if he misses, he tumbles off himself. And how quiet the horses are! They let them on and off just as if they were tables."

Another Rule of Battle seemed to be that they always fell on their heads. The battle ended when they both fell off. Then they shook hands and the Red Knight rode away.

"It was a glorious victory, wasn't it?" the White Knight panted.

"I don't know," said Alice. "I don't want to be a prisoner. I want to be a Queen!"

"So you will be when you've crossed the next brook," said the White Knight. "I'll see you safe to the end of the wood, then I must go back. That's the end of my move."

"Thank you very much," said Alice. "Can I help you off with your helmet?"

He was dressed in badly fitting armour, with a queer little wooden box fastened across his shoulders upside down, with the lid hanging open.

The battle ended when they both fell off.

"I see you're admiring my little box," smiled the Knight. "It's my own invention. I keep clothes and sandwiches in it and carry it upside down, so the rain can't get in."

"But the things can get out," said Alice. "Do you know the lid's open?"

"I didn't know it," the Knight said. "Then all the things must have fallen out!" He was about to throw the box away. Instead he hung it carefully on a tree. "Can you guess why I did that?" he asked Alice. She shook her head. "In hopes that bees may nest in it, then I should get the honey."

"But you've got a beehive fastened to the saddle," said Alice.

"Yes, a good one, but not a single bee has come near it yet. And the other thing is a mousetrap. The mice keep the bees out, or the bees keep the mice out, I don't know which. You see, it's as well to be provided for everything. What's that dish for?"

"It's meant for plum-cake," said Alice.

"We'd better take it with us," the Knight said. "It'll come in handy if we find any. I hope you've got your hair well fastened on?" he continued as they set off.

"Only in the usual way," Alice said, smiling.

"That's hardly enough," he said anxiously. "The wind is so *very* strong. But I've got a plan for keeping it from falling off. You take an upright stick, then make your hair creep up it, like a fruit tree. The reason hair falls off is because it hangs down. Things never fall upwards, you know."

Alice thought about this as she walked, every now and then stopping to help the poor Knight, who was *not* a good rider and kept falling off. "I'm afraid you've not had much practice in riding," she said, helping him up from his fifth tumble.

The Knight looked offended as he scrambled back into the saddle, holding Alice's hair to save himself from falling over

"I'm afraid you've not had much practice in riding."

the other side. "The art of good riding," he said, falling heavily on his head, "is the art of balance!"

"This is ridiculous. You ought to have a wooden horse," said Alice, "on wheels!"

"I'll get one," said the Knight thoughtfully. "One, two, or several." There was a short silence, then the Knight went on, "I'm quite good at inventing things, you know. Would you like to hear a new way to get over a gate?"

"Very much indeed," said Alice politely.

"You see," said the Knight, "the only difficulty is the feet. The head is high enough already. So I put my head on the top of the gate . . . then the head's high enough, then I stand on my head . . . then the feet are high enough . . . then I'm over, you see?"

"Don't you think it would be rather hard?" said Alice.

"I haven't tried it yet," said the Knight gravely, "so I can't tell for certain." He raised his hand as he said this and rolled out of the saddle and fell headlong into a deep ditch "But I'm afraid it would be a *little* hard."

"How can you go on talking, head downwards?" Alice asked, as she dragged him out by his feet.

"What does it matter where my body happens to be?" he said. "My mind goes on working all the same. In fact, the more head downwards I am, the more I keep inventing things."

Alice looked puzzled.

"You look sad," the Knight said. "Let me sing you a song to comfort you."

"Is it long?" Alice asked, for she had heard a lot of poetry that day.

"It's long," said the Knight, "but it's very beautiful. The song is called *A-sitting on a gate*, and the tune's my own invention." So saying, he stopped his horse, for they had reached the end of the wood, and with a faint smile lighting his gentle, foolish face, he began.

Of all the strange things Alice saw on her journey through the Looking-glass, this was the one she always remembered most clearly. The mild blue eyes and kindly smile of the Knight, the setting sun blazing on his armour, the horse quietly moving, reins dangling, and the black shadows of the forest behind. She leaned against a tree, watching and listening in a half dream to the melancholy music of the song. ("But the tune isn't his own invention," she thought. "I've heard it before.")

"I'll tell thee everything I can;
  There's little to relate.
I saw an aged aged man,
  A-sitting on a gate.
'Who are you, aged man?' I said.
  'And how is it you live?'
And his answer trickled through my head,
  Like water through a sieve.

He said 'I look for butterflies
  That sleep among the wheat:
I make them into mutton-pies,
  And sell them in the street.
I sell them unto men,' he said,
  'Who sail on stormy seas;
And that's the way I get my bread—
  A trifle, if you please.'

But I was thinking of a plan
  To dye one's whiskers green,
And always use so large a fan
  That they could not be seen.
So, having no reply to give
  To what the old man said,
I cried 'Come, tell me how you live!'
  And thumped him on the head.

His accents mild took up the tale:
  He said 'I go my ways,
And when I find a mountain-rill,
  I set it in a blaze;
And thence they make a stuff they call
  Rowland's Macassar Oil—
Yet twopence-halfpenny is all
  They give me for my toil.'

I saw an aged aged man, A-sitting on a gate.

But I was thinking of a way
    To feed oneself on batter,
And so go on from day to day
    Getting a little fatter.
I shook him well from side to side,
    Until his face was blue:
'Come, tell me how you live,' I cried,
    'And what it is you do!'

He said 'I hunt for haddocks' eyes
    Among the heather bright,
And work them into waistcoat-buttons
    In the silent night.
And these I do not sell for gold
    Or coin of silvery shine,
But for a copper halfpenny,
    And that will purchase nine.

'I sometimes dig for buttered rolls,
    Or set limed twigs for crabs:
I sometimes search the grassy knolls
    For wheels of Hansom-cabs.
And that's the way' (he gave a wink)
    'By which I get my wealth—
And very gladly will I drink
    Your Honour's noble health.'

I heard him then, for I had just
    Completed my design
To keep the Menai bridge from rust
    By boiling it in wine.
I thanked him much for telling me
    The way he got his wealth,
But chiefly for his wish that he
    Might drink my noble health.

And now, if e'er by chance I put
    My fingers into glue,
Or madly squeeze a right-hand foot
    Into a left-hand shoe,
Or if I drop upon my toe
    A very heavy weight,
I weep, for it reminds me so
Of that old man I used to know—
Who look was mild, whose speech was slow,
Whose hair was whiter than the snow,
Whose face was very like a crow,
With eyes, like cinders, all aglow,
Who seemed distracted with his woe,
Who rocked his body to and fro,
And muttered mumblingly and low,
As if his mouth were full of dough,
Who snorted like a buffalo—
That summer evening long ago,
    A-sitting on a gate."

As the Knight sang the last words of the ballad, he gathered up the reins, and turned his horse's head. "You've only a few yards to go," he said. "Down the hill and over that little brook and then you'll be a Queen."

"Thank you," said Alice and they shook hands, "for coming so far, and I liked your song very much."

"I hope so," said the Knight doubtfully and then rode slowly away.

"There he goes," thought Alice. "Right on his head as usual. But how easily he climbs back on!" She waited till he was out of sight, then turned, and ran down the hill. "And now for the last brook, and to be a Queen. The Eighth Square at last!" she cried, as she

bounded over and threw herself down to rest on a lawn as soft as moss. "Oh, how glad I am to get here! And what is this?" She put her hands up to something very heavy that fitted tight round her head. "How can it possibly . . .?"

It was a golden crown.

CHAPTER 9

Queen Alice

"Well, this is grand!" said Alice. "I never expected I should be a Queen so soon. And if I really am a Queen, I shall manage it quite well in time."

Everything was happening so oddly that she didn't feel a bit surprised at finding the Red Queen and the White Queen sitting next to her. There would be no harm, she thought, in asking if the game was over. "Please –" she began, looking timidly at the Red Queen.

"Speak when you're spoken to!" the Red Queen sharply interrupted her.

"But if everybody obeyed that rule, nobody would ever say anything –"

"Ridiculous!" cried the Red Queen, with a frown. She thought for a minute, then suddenly changed the subject. "What do you mean by 'If you really are a Queen'? You can't be a Queen till you've passed the proper examinations."

"I only said 'if'!" Alice pleaded.

The two Queens looked at each other. "She says she only said 'if'!" the Red Queen remarked.

"I didn't mean –" Alice was beginning, when the Red Queen interrupted.

"That's just what I complain of! You *should* have meant," and there was an uncomfortable silence for a minute or two.

The Red Queen broke the silence by saying to the White

Queen, "I invite you to Alice's dinner-party this afternoon."

The White Queen smiled feebly, and said, "And I invite *you*."

"I didn't know I was going to have a party," said Alice. "But if I am, then surely I should invite the guests?"

"We gave you the opportunity," the Red Queen remarked, "but I dare say you've not had many lessons in manners yet?"

"Manners are not taught in lessons," said Alice. "Lessons teach you to do sums and the like."

"Can you do Addition?" the White Queen asked. "What's one and one and one and one and one and one?"

"I don't know," said Alice. "I lost count."

"She can't do Addition," the Red Queen interrupted. "Can you do Subtraction? Take nine from eight!"

"I can't," Alice began, "but –"

"She can't do Subtraction," said the White Queen. "Can you do Division? Divide a loaf by a knife – what's the answer to that?"

"I suppose –" Alice was beginning, but the Red Queen answered for her.

"Bread and butter, of course. She can't do sums a bit!"

"Can *you* do sums?" Alice turned on the White Queen, who gasped and shut her eyes.

"I can do Addition, but not Subtraction under *any* circumstances!"

"Of course you know your ABC?" said the Red Queen.

"To be sure I do," said Alice.

"So do I," the White Queen whispered. "I can read words of one letter!"

"Fan her head!" the Red Queen interrupted. "She'll be feverish after so much thinking." So they set to work, and fanned her with bunches of leaves, till she begged them to leave off. "She's all right now," said the Red Queen. "What's the cause of lightning?"

"Fan her head!" the Red Queen interrupted.

"Thunder is the cause of lightning," said Alice firmly. "No, no, I meant the other way round . . ." She couldn't help thinking to herself, "What dreadful nonsense we are talking."

"Too late to correct it!" said the Red Queen. "Which reminds me, we had a thunderstorm on one of the last set of Tuesdays."

"In our country," Alice remarked, "we only have one Tuesday at a time."

"That's a poor way of doing things," the Red Queen said. "Here we have days and nights two or three at a time."

"It was *such* a thunderstorm, you can't think," the White Queen said. "And part of the roof came off, and ever so much thunder got in . . . it went rolling round the room in great lumps, knocking over tables and things, till I was so frightened, I couldn't remember my own name." The White Queen gave a deep sigh, and laid her head on Alice's shoulder. "I *am* so sleepy," she moaned.

"She's tired, poor thing," said the Red Queen. "Lend her your nightcap and sing her a lullaby."

"I haven't got a nightcap," said Alice. "And I don't know any lullabies."

"I must do it myself, then," said the Red Queen, and she began:

> "Hush-a-by lady, in Alice's lap!
>   Till the feast's ready, we've time for a nap.
> When the feast's over, we'll go to the ball,
>   Red Queen and White Queen and Alice and all!"

"And now you know the words," she added, putting her head on Alice's other shoulder. "Sing it to *me*. I'm getting sleepy too." In a moment, both Queens were fast asleep, snoring loud.

"What *am* I to do?" exclaimed Alice perplexed, as first one head, then the other, rolled from her shoulder and lay like a heavy lump in her lap. The snoring grew louder every minute and sounded like a tune. She listened so eagerly, she hardly noticed the two heads vanish from her lap.

She was standing before an arched doorway, over which

were the words QUEEN ALICE Just then, the door opened and a creature with a long beak put its head out and said, "No admittance till the week after next!" and shut the door again with a bang.

Alice knocked in vain and at last a very old Frog, who was sitting under a tree, hobbled towards her. He was dressed in yellow, with very large boots. "What is it now?" the Frog whispered.

Alice turned round. "Where is the servant whose business it is to answer the door?" she began angrily.

"Which door?" said the Frog.

Alice stamped her foot. "This door, of course!"

The Frog looked at the door, then rubbed it with his thumb, as if testing the paint. "Answer the door?" he said. "What's it been asking?"

"Nothing!" Alice said impatiently. "I've been knocking at it!"

"Shouldn't do that," the Frog muttered. "Annoys it, you know!" Then he gave the door a kick with one of his great feet. "You let it alone," he panted, "and it'll let you alone." At this moment, the door was flung open, and a shrill voice was heard singing:

"To the Looking-glass world it was Alice that said
'I've a sceptre in hand, I've a crown on my head.
Let the Looking-glass creatures, whatever they be,
Come and dine with the Red Queen, the White Queen and me!'"

Alice glanced nervously along the table, as she walked up the large hall. She noticed guests of all kinds: animals, birds, even a few flowers. There were three chairs at the head of the table; the Red Queen and the White Queen had taken two of them, so Alice sat down in the middle one.

The Red Queen spoke. "You've missed the soup and fish," she said. "Put on the joint!" And the waiters set a leg of mutton before Alice.

"Answer the door?" he said. "What's it been asking?"

"You look shy. Let me introduce you," said the Red Queen. "Alice – Mutton; Mutton – Alice." The leg of mutton got up in the dish, and made a little bow to Alice.

"May I give you a slice?" said Alice, taking up the knife.

"Certainly not!" the Red Queen said. "It isn't polite to cut anyone you've been introduced to." The waiters removed the mutton, and brought a large plum-pudding.

"I won't be introduced to the pudding, please," Alice said quickly, "or we'll get no dinner!"

But the Red Queen growled, "Alice – Pudding; Pudding – Alice. Remove the pudding!" and the waiters took it away. However, Alice didn't see why the Red Queen should be the only one to give orders, so she called out, "Waiter! Bring back the pudding!" and there it was again. She cut a slice and handed it to the Red Queen.

There was dead silence, then Alice said, "Do you know, I've heard so much poetry today, and much of it about fishes. Do you know why they're so fond of fishes all about here?"

"Her White Majesty," the Red Queen said solemnly, "knows a lovely poem about fishes. Shall she repeat it?"

"May I?" the White Queen cooed.

"Please do!" said Alice politely, and the White Queen began:

> *"'First, the fish must be caught.'*
> *That is easy: a baby, I think, could have caught it.*
> *'Next, the fish must be bought.'*
> *That is easy: a penny, I think, would have bought it.*
>
> *'Now cook me the fish!'*
> *That is easy, and will not take more than a minute.*
> *'Let it lie in a dish!'*
> *That is easy, because it already is in it.*

> *'Bring it here! Let me sup!'*
> *It is easy to set such a dish on the table.*
> *'Take the dish-cover up!'*
> *Ah, that is so hard that I fear I'm unable!*
>
> *For it holds it like glue—*
> *Holds the lid to the dish, while it lies in the middle.*
> *Which is easiest to do,*
> *Un-dish-cover the fish, or dishcover the riddle?"*

"Think about it!" said the Red Queen. "Meanwhile, we'll drink your health. Queen Alice's health" she screamed.

All the guests began drinking, and queerly so. Some of them put their glasses on their heads and drank all that trickled down their faces. Others upset the decanters and drank what ran off the table. Three kangaroo-like creatures scrambled into the dish of mutton and lapped up the gravy.

"You ought to return thanks in a speech," the Red Queen said, frowning.

It was difficult to make a speech, between the two Queens, who pushed her so that she nearly rose into the air. "I rise to return thanks –" Alice began, and she really *did* rise as she spoke, but she got hold of the table, and pulled herself down.

"Take care!" screamed the White Queen. "Something's going to happen!"

Then, all sorts of things did happen. The candles grew up to the ceiling and the bottles each took a pair of plates as wings, and so, with forks for legs, went fluttering about.

Alice heard a hoarse laugh at her side, and turned to see the leg of mutton sitting in the White Queen's chair.

"Here I am!" cried a voice from the soup tureen and Alice saw the Queen's good-natured face grinning at her, before she disappeared into the soup.

"I can't stand this any longer!" she cried.

"I can't stand this any longer!" Alice cried, as she seized the tablecloth with both hands: one good pull and plates, dishes, guests and candles came crashing down together in a heap on the floor.

"And as for *you*," she went on, turning fiercely on the Red Queen, whom she considered the cause of all the mischief, but the Queen was no longer at her side. She had dwindled to the size of a little doll and was running round the table.

"As for *you*," she repeated, catching hold of the little creature, "I'll shake you into a kitten, that I will!"

CHAPTER 10

Shaking

S he took her off the table as she spoke and shook her backwards and forwards with all her might.

The Red Queen made no resistance whatever; only her face grew very small, and her eyes got large and green: and still, as Alice went on shaking her, she kept on growing shorter – and fatter – and softer – and rounder – and –

CHAPTER 11
Waking

– and it really was a kitten, after all.

CHAPTER 12

Which Dreamed It?

"Your Red Majesty shouldn't purr so loud," Alice said, rubbing her eyes. "You woke me out of . . . oh, such a nice dream! And you've been along with me, Kitty – all through the Looking-glass world. Did you know it, dear?"

The kitten only purred, and it was impossible to know if it meant 'yes' or 'no'.

So Alice hunted through the chessmen on the table, and found the Red Queen. She went down on her knees and put the kitten and the Queen to look at each other. "Now, Kitty," she cried, "you've got to confess that that was what you turned into! Sit up a little more stiffly, dear!" Alice laughed.

"And curtsey while you're thinking what to purr." She gave the kitten a little kiss.

"Snowdrop, my pet!" she went on, looking at the white kitten, who was still undergoing its toilet. "When will Dinah finish with your White Majesty? Dinah, do you know you're scrubbing a White Queen?" She prattled on, "And what did you turn to, Dinah? Were you Humpty Dumpty? By the way, Kitty, if you'd *really* been in my dream, you would have enjoyed all the poetry about fishes. Tomorrow morning you shall have a real treat, while you're eating your breakfast. I'll repeat *The Walrus and the Carpenter* to you, then you can pretend it's oysters.

"Now, Kitty, let's consider who it was that dreamed it all. You see, Kitty, it must have been either me or the Red King. He was part of my dream, but then, I was part of his, too. *Was* it the Red King, Kitty? You were his wife, so you ought to know. Oh, Kitty, *do* help me settle it!" But the kitten pretended not to hear.

. . . Which do *you* think it was?

A boat beneath a sunny sky,
Lingering onwards dreamily
In an evening of July –

Children three that nestle near,
Eager eye and willing ear,
Pleased a simple tale to hear –

Long has paled that sunny sky:
Echoes fade and memories die:
Autumn frosts have slain July.

Still she haunts me, phantomwise,
Alice moving under skies
Never seen by waking eyes.

Children yet, the tale to hear,
Eager eye and willing ear,
Lovingly shall nestle near.

In a Wonderland they lie,
Dreaming as the days go by,
Dreaming as the summers die.

Ever drifting down the stream –
Lingering in the golden gleam –
Life, what is it but a dream?